Postman Pat
Makes a Splash

Story by **John Cunliffe**
Pictures by **Joan Hickson**

From the original Television designs by **Ivor Wood**

André Deutsch/Hippo Books

Published simultaneously in hardback by
André Deutsch Limited,
105-106 Great Russell Street, London WC1B 3LJ
and in paperback by Hippo Books, Scholastic Publications Limited,
10 Earlham Street, London WC2H 9RX in 1987

Reprinted 1987

Text copyright © 1987 John Cunliffe
Illustrations copyright © 1987 by André Deutsch Limited,
Scholastic Publications Limited
and Woodland Animations Limited

ISBN 0 233 98119 5 (hardback)
ISBN 0 590 70753 1 (paperback)

Made and printed in Belgium by Proost
Typeset in Plantin by Span Graphics, London

There was a new baby at Greendale
Farm.

Baby Paul.

One hot summer day, Pat and Jess
called with the letters.

Baby Paul was having a lovely time.

He was sitting in his yellow plastic
baby bath, in a sunny place in the
garden.

Paul loved the water.

He splashed and shouted.

Mrs. Pottage tickled his tummy.

Paul laughed and gurgled.

He loved his plastic duck.

In the pond, the real ducks splashed.
They quacked and quacked. They
loved the water. Just like Baby Paul.

"Good morning!" said Pat, coming with the letters. "What a nice day for a swim. Is there room for me?"

"I don't think you'd fit in," said Mrs. Pottage.

"Goo goo, guggle,". said Paul.

"Quite right," said Pat.

"What about Jess?" said Mrs. Pottage. "Would Jess like a paddle?"

Jess hid. He hated the water.

There was a shout from the yard.
"Quick! Quick! Catch it! Look out!"
There was a tip tap of feet, running
across the yard. There was a clump
clump of boots running across the yard.
Who was it?

Pat ran to the garden gate.

"My goodness!" said Pat. "It's your pig! It's run away! And Peter Fogg's after it."

"It'll be that Jenny again," said Mrs. Pottage. "Oh, she is a demon! She's forever running away. And Peter will never catch her by himself."

"I'll go and give him a hand," said Pat.

"No," said Mrs. Pottage, "I know that
pig better than anyone. She'll behave
for me. Oh, Pat, could you see to Paul?
Just dry him and put his nappy on? I'll
catch that pig in a minute."

"Leave it to me," said Pat. "I'm sure I
can manage a baby better than a pig."

Pat held Paul in his baby bath.

Mrs. Pottage ran after the pig.

Jess came to see what was going on.

Paul laughed and splashed in his baby
bath.

"No more splashing," said Pat, "I'm
getting wet."

Paul didn't know what Pat said. He was too small. He splashed and splashed.

"Oh dear," said Pat. "I'm getting very wet."

Jess watched. He didn't come too near. He didn't want to get wet.

"You'd better come out now," said Pat. But Paul didn't want to come out of the water. He kicked when Pat tried to lift him out. He kicked and splashed. Pat got wetter and wetter.

"Come and help me, Jess," said Pat.
Jess stood where Paul could see him,
and said, "Miaow."
Paul looked at Jess.
Paul said, "Ooo goo esss."
He stopped kicking. He liked Jess. He
wanted to play with Jess.

"You can play with Jess," said Pat,
"when you're dry. Jess doesn't like
water."
Paul kept still.
Pat lifted him on to the towel.
He wrapped the towel round him. He
dried him all over.
Now Jess came to Paul.

"That's right," said Pat. "Stroke Jess nicely. Now let's see about this nappy. Keep still, Paul. Now, let's see; how on earth do you put a nappy on?"

Dear me, what a time Pat had with
that nappy! He thought it would be like
making a parcel.
It wasn't.

Parcels keep still. Babies don't.

Paul wriggled and giggled. He thought it was all a big joke. He just wouldn't keep still. Every time Pat got the nappy on, Paul kicked it off again. Pat got the nappy on at last, and he couldn't find the safety-pin!

Then the garden gate flew open. The pig ran into the garden, with Mrs. Pottage and Peter Fogg after it. It went

through a flower-bed, knocked the
dustbin over, broke two milk-bottles, and
ran out through the hedge.

And what a squealing it made!
The hen and her chicks went and hid
behind the rockery.
The foal galloped over and looked over
the hedge to see what was going on.

Mrs. Pottage caught the pig at last, by rattling a bucket full of mash. She thought it was feeding time, but soon found out it wasn't!

"I need a bath and a brush after that,"
said Mrs. Pottage, when she came
back. "Now let's see how Pat and Paul
are getting on."
How she smiled when she saw them!

Pat was sitting with a crumpled
nappy in his hand. He looked
very tired.

Paul was playing with Jess.
He had given Jess his woolly ball to
play with. He was laughing and
gurgling at him. They were having a
lovely time.

"Hm," said Mrs. Pottage. "You didn't
get far with the nappy, did you?"

"Dearie me," said Pat, "he just would not keep still."

"Well, he likes playing with nothing on," said Mrs. Pottage, "and he's having a lovely time with Jess. But we'd better get his nappy on, now. You just have to be firm, you know."

A puff of talc, and a few squeals later, Paul was well tucked into his nappy and his clothes.

"I must say," said Mrs. Pottage, "you two make very good baby-sitters. I'll take the letters round, and you can look after Paul for the day."

"I think I'll stick to letters," said Pat. "I'm better at that. I'd better be on my way, now."

"Thanks for keeping an eye on Paul," said Mrs. Pottage. "I don't know what we would have done without you. Cheerio!"

"I think Jess helped more than I did," said Pat. "Bye!"

At lunchtime, Pat put his hand in his pocket and found a piece of soap and a safety-pin. The soap was furry from the fluff in his pocket.

And next time he had to wrap a parcel,

he found it ever so easy.